Bloomsbury Publishing, London, Berlin and New York

First published in Great Britain in 2009 by Bloomsbury Publishing Plc
36 Soho Square, London, W1D 3QY

A CIP catalogue record of this book is available from the British Library

ISBN 978 0 7475 9827 5

1 3 5 7 9 10 8 6 4 2

Printed in Great Britain by Clays Ltd, St Ives Plc

The paper this book is printed on is certified independently in accordance
with the rules of the FSC. It is ancient-forest friendly.
The printer holds chain of custody.

Mixed Sources
Product group from well-managed
forests and other controlled sources
www.fsc.org Cert no. SGS-COC-2061
© 1996 Forest Stewardship Council

FSC

www.bloomsbury.com

Knife and Packer

BLOOMSBURY

LONDON BERLIN NEW YORK

ZAC ZOLTAN'S
MAD MONSTER
AGENCY

Meet Josh Flunk – a regular school kid.	And his best friend, Spencer Topps.

They live in the town of Everyday, which is an everyday kind of place. Except . . . unlike most towns Everyday has a DARK side. From time to time phantoms creep and spectres loom. But these aren't your common, everyday monsters, these are MAD monsters and they are REAL!

Getting rid of them requires much more than an 'everyday' solution. Time to find out about the Mad Monster Agency.

When Josh Flunk's great-great-great-grandfather, Franklin Flunk, bought an ancient Egyptian sarcophagus from a junk shop, he didn't realise it was going to change his life, and his family's life, for ever . . .

When Franklin took it home and dusted it down, he noticed that an object had been left at the back.

He stepped inside to discover a bizarre walking stick with an ivory skull-shaped handle that had fiery rubies for eyes . . .

And that's when the lid slammed shut behind him. There was an eerie moaning, a strange glow and then a loud BANG!

When Franklin stepped out he had transformed into ZEBADIAH ZOLTAN – MAD MONSTER AGENT extraordinaire!

From that day on, every time the eyes on the walking stick started to glow it meant there was a Mad Monster crisis.

The Mad Monster Agency passed down the generations, until Josh's father was mauled by a zombie mouse and developed a phobia for all things monster. The next in line was, you guessed it . . .

Franklin Flunk would hurry to the secret room he had built beneath his house, step into the sarcophagus, and become Zebadiah Zoltan once more – ready to protect the town of Everyday.

HOORAH!

Josh Flunk, aka Zac Zoltan, the latest (and youngest ever) head of the Mad Monster Agency!

ZAP!

Along with his partner, Spencer Topps, alias the gadget king, Dr Brains . . .

And trusty assistant and Troll, Odd Dan the Odd . . .

Zac Zoltan fearlessly fights Mad Monsters of all sizes (and shapes).

Although there are lots of imitators . . .

AUNTY EDITH's NASTY MONSTER SORTING-OUT ORGANISATION

there is only one MAD MONSTER AGENCY.

In fact a Mad Monster might just be stirring at this very moment . . .

Chapter One of . . .

1

Trips with Everyday School weren't usually much fun. But as the school coach pulled into the long, tree-lined road leading to the Everyday Archaeological Museum on the outskirts of town, Josh and Spencer immediately felt that this one might be something special . . .

'I wonder what they could have dug up here?' whispered Josh. 'I'm sensing something not quite right about this place.'

'Hello and welcome,' said a small, neat lady in a uniform. 'My name is Irma Sneef and along with my husband, Irving Sneef, I own and run Everyday's only archaeological museum. I will be your guide today.' She paused, cleared her throat dramatically, then continued, 'We bought this land to build our retirement home on, but when the bathroom sank into the ground we realised this field hid something extraordinary . . .

'As the fireman rescued me from my bath, we had no idea that what we were about to discover was the ruins of an ancient civilisation!'

'You mean like the Mayans or the Ancient Egyptians?' piped up Spencer, who considered himself to be a bit of an expert on early civilisations. (In fact he considered himself to be a bit of an expert on just about everything.)

'Earlier than that,' said Mrs Sneef haughtily. 'You've heard of the Bronze Age and the Iron Age. Yes, but did you know that in between there was a short period that we have named . . . THE CHOCOLATE AGE? Let me explain.'

'These primitive people were the first to discover how to make chocolate! Using crude tools they made the first chocolate bars, the first chocolate biscuits and even pioneered early chocolate ice cream . . .'

'They soon became wealthy and built a highly advanced settlement.'

'But then all of a sudden they disappeared – we still don't know why . . .'

'The Chocolate Age!' marvelled Josh. 'Now that sounds like my kind of age.'

'We believe the origins of the annual Everyday Chocolate Festival go all the way back to those times,' said Mrs Sneef. 'We are going to start the visit at part of the site which has only recently been excavated, so you will all have to wear protective overalls and masks.'

'I presume we may well encounter ancient pollens and toxins unearthed by the digging process,' said Spencer, who was so brainy Josh sometimes wondered how he could fit everything in one head.

As the tour started, it didn't take long for Mrs Sneef to grab everyone's attention.

'At its peak the people of the Chocolate Age produced enough chocolate here to fill an Olympic-sized swimming pool – every day!'

'We believe this is where the cocoa beans were processed. And this is where the chocolate was stored.'

'Where we're standing now would have been the marketplace where the chocolate was sold.'

'Wow!' said Josh. 'This place must have been amazing. I wonder what happened.'

'There are no signs of a natural disaster,' said Spencer, scrutinising the ground. 'It must have been something catastrophic.'

'Follow me,' said Mrs Sneef, as they proceeded back through to the museum. 'You are about to see the most prized artefact in the whole collection – only recently discovered, and on display to the public for the very first time!'

She led them into a small, dark room off the main visitor area.

2

'Behold the Amulet of Nutty Knitty!'

In a glass case was a primitive medallion made entirely of chocolate, sprinkled with what looked like ancient hazelnuts!

'We think this is the world's oldest surviving item of confectionery,' said Mrs Sneef. 'It was found in a secret cavern deep beneath the ground.'

'What does it have written on it?' asked Josh.

'I believe that's an ancient language, not used for many centuries,' said Spencer. 'The grammar is clearly of a defunct variety.'

'We are currently researching the meaning of the inscription,' hissed Mrs Sneef, who didn't like clever kids. 'We do, however, know what it says: Knit Nutty, Nut Knitty, Nut, Nut, NUTS!'

'No one knows exactly why the Chocolate Age ended so abruptly. But legend tells of an ancient curse . . .' she continued. 'And it's possible the Amulet holds a valuable clue. That's why it's kept under lock and key. We wouldn't want anyone taking a bite out of it . . .' she added mysteriously.

'Ancient curse?!?' scoffed a loud voice from the back of the group. 'Let ME have a closer look!'

It was Boyston Fitch, the school bully, (who also happened to be quite brainless).

'I'm going to have a bite of your stupid old chocolate right here, right now!' continued Boyston. 'We'll soon see if it's CURSED.'

Before their teacher could stop him Boyston pushed past Mrs Sneef to the display case and yanked at the handle.

'That case is alarmed!' shrieked their guide. 'Stop at once!'

But Boyston wasn't listening – a loud ringing noise erupted, followed by a torrential shower of water from the ceiling. Boyston was drenched!

'I did warn you,' tutted Mrs Sneef. 'Of course we don't believe in curses! We'd simply like to keep the Amulet safe from hungry visitors.'

Before anyone could ask any more questions she hurried them on to the next exhibit.

'Cursed amulets, a Chocolate Age coming to a mysterious end . . . and Boyston getting soaked!' said Josh, when they were back on the school bus. 'Well, that was certainly more fun than the last school trip.'

'Yes, although I actually found the visit to the Everyday Business Conference Centre quite interesting too,' said Spencer.

'Why?!?' asked Josh, who was always surprised by what his best friend found exciting.

'Come on, there was all sorts of great stuff there: lecterns, overhead projectors, and all those trade conferences,' said Spencer.

'Trade conferences?' exclaimed Josh. 'What was the one they were getting ready for? Oh yes, the dentists' conference!'

'Dentistry is underrated,' protested Spencer. But before he could describe what he found interesting about drills and mouthwash the bus pulled up in front of their school.

3

Josh and Spencer went straight back to Josh's house.

'So how was the trip to the museum?' asked Josh's mum. 'Of course, I consider *myself* to be a bit of an amateur archaeologist.'

'Really?' asked Spencer. 'Have you discovered any fascinating artefacts?'

'I specialise in the Messy Kid Age,' said Mrs Flunk. 'I'm always digging up ancient socks and underwear in Josh's room.'

'Mum!' said Josh, embarrassed. 'I'll go and tidy it now . . .'

But as soon as they entered Josh's bedroom Josh and Spencer froze. Leaning in the corner was Josh's great-great-great-grandfather's walking stick . . . and the eyes on the ivory skull were glowing red! Josh and Spencer glanced at each other knowingly. This was the signal to go to the Mad Monster Agency.

They crawled under the bed as fast as they could . . . past old toys, dustballs and a particularly grubby plimsoll.

'You know, you really should tidy up under here,' said Spencer as he came face to face with a discarded pair of pants. 'The common dust mite is responsible for most allergies.'

'Some of my best friends are dust mites,' said Josh as he wormed his way round an old pair of trainers.

They reached a loose floorboard. Josh gave a coded series of taps and a hidden trapdoor slid back to reveal a steep chute leading down into the secret room.
Josh and Spencer slipped through the opening feet first. At the foot of the slide was the entrance to the ancient Egyptian sarcophagus.

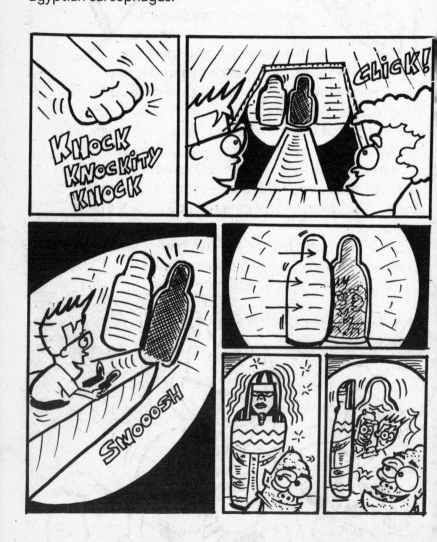

Once they were inside, it began to work its magic. The sarcophagus wobbled and throbbed, then there was a loud BANG. Josh had transformed into Zac Zoltan, Mad Monster special agent! And Spencer was now Mad Monster gadget expert Dr Brains!

But instead of a Mad Monster Crisis what they faced was a strong smell of baking.

'I hope you're hungry,' chuckled a deep voice from the back of the office.

'Odd Dan,' sighed Zac, 'you know the ivory skull is only to be activated in an emergency!'

'Sorry,' said Odd Dan. 'It's been so quiet around here lately. And I've been baking your favourite biscuits.'

MAD MONSTER AGENCY FACT FILE:

FULL NAME: Odd Dan the Odd, son of Odd Stan the Weird and Odd Jan the Even Weirder.

TYPE: Cake-Baking Troll. A type of Troll that specialises in making sponges, puddings and biscuits. Not to be messed with, these Trolls are experts in the ancient martial art of Kung Food, where everyday food items are used in self-defence (Odd Dan is particularly handy with a chocolate chip cookie).

AGE: 878 years old.

SPECIALITY: Huge knowledge of Mad Monsters and their habits — the more nutty, deranged or round the bend the monsters are, the more he knows about them.

ODD DAN FACT: Zac and Dr Brains first met Odd Dan on a previous mission — **Attack of the Cake-Baking Trolls**. When they had successfully defeated the Troll-pack, one Troll was left behind, stuck in a giant Victoria sponge of his own baking. Too embarrassed to rejoin the other Trolls, Odd Dan decided to mend his ways. He became Josh and Spencer's friend and has been the Agency's resident Mad Monster Expert ever since . . . as well as housekeeper and receptionist. When he can be dragged away from his duster and oven, he helps Zac Zoltan and Dr Brains on missions and drives the Mad Monstermobile.

After Odd Dan had promised to activate the ivory skull only when there was a genuine monster emergency, Zac started to pick his brains.

'There's something strange about the place we visited on our school trip today,' said Zac, eating a biscuit and handing Odd Dan the museum brochure. 'Have you ever heard of it?'

'The Chocolate Age settlement?' said Odd Dan, scratching his large chin.

Although Odd Dan's knowledge of Mad Monster history was second to none, he always had to eat biscuits to really get his brain working. Munching on a double fudge shortcake, he started muttering about creatures and haunted places.

'Ah, the Cheese Monkeys of Borneo. Nasty little critters,' said Odd Dan.

'Haunted mayonnaise factories, bicycle shop ghouls, and . . . yes . . . the Everyday Chocolate Settlement.'

'Have you remembered something?' asked Zac hopefully.

'It was a terrible time!' answered Odd Dan dramatically. 'Once it was a thriving community, but then disaster struck.'

'Disaster?' said Zac.

'What happened to the creatures?' asked Zac.

'They were finally captured by the last few surviving inhabitants and buried in a biscuit urn for eternity. People knew more about Mad Monsters back then,' said Odd Dan, pointing to a picture of the Amulet of Nutty Knitty in the brochure. 'The Amulet is what they employed to magically seal the urn. If the Amulet is so much as nibbled, the creatures will be freed and no one's snacks will ever be safe again!'

But that still doesn't explain why so many people just 'disappeared'. I think there's something more to these creatures . .

Meanwhile, at the Everyday Archaeological Museum, a new member of staff was starting his first day. Because the place was so creepy, the Sneefs always had problems finding nightwatchmen willing to guard it. So they were delighted to discover Gerard Snax, an enthusiastic insomniac. What they didn't realise was that Gerard also had a burning passion for all things chocolatey . . .

Mr Lardo's Choc-Fudge Delight

'Welcome, Gerard. I see that Mrs Sneef told you to bring a torch. Good, good,' said Irving Sneef, as he showed the new recruit around the museum. 'Make sure you circulate between all the rooms.'

'Will do,' said Gerard.

'There's a TV in your office, so in between patrols feel free to enjoy some late-night television,' continued Irving Sneef. 'But there is something I must warn you about.'

'Really? What's that?' asked Gerard, intrigued.

'Oh, that won't be a problem,' said Gerard. 'I'm prepared.'
The new nightwatchman opened up his jacket to reveal dozens of concealed pockets, each containing a chocolate bar.

'Well, you have been warned,' said Mr Sneef.
With Mr and Mrs Sneef and the rest of the staff gone, Gerard was left to get on with the job of protecting the site. At first all went well . . . He patrolled the museum, ate the occasional snack from his jacket, then watched some late-night television. But one room kept on drawing him back . . .

'Mmm, the Amulet!' thought Gerard, his mouth watering. 'It's thousands of years old but it looks like it was made only yesterday. And it's so very, very tempting.'

  Before he knew it, Gerard was kneeling in front of the display case. He was starting to drool.

'Look at those ancient nuts! Behold the rich, aged chocolate . . .' Suddenly he realised what he was doing. He remembered the snacks in his jacket and as he grabbed a hazelnut surprise from one of the hidden pockets and hurried back to his office, he noticed he was sweating . . .

Unaware of developments at the museum, Josh and Spencer had other things on their minds. At school excitement was mounting.

Each year, on one special day, Everyday celebrated the town's chocolate heritage. There were chocolate-making competitions and chocolate stands boasting exotic chocolates, and the finest chocolate-makers in the world would show off their latest creations. And, of course, there was the highlight of the festival: the Chocolate Parade, with spectacular floats made by the residents of Everyday. There was a prize for the best float and competition was fierce . . .

Josh and Spencer had almost finished work on their float –
a giant chocolate dinosaur: the Chocosaurus.

'Our dinosaur has got to have a great chance of winning,'
said Josh, admiring their handiwork.

'I had to use all my knowledge of construction
engineering to get those horns to stick on,' said Spencer,
tapping away at a calculator. 'This beauty could survive a
hurricane.'

Spencer had worked hard on the horns because of what had happened at last year's Chocolate Festival . . .

'Hey, losers,' came a familiar and unpleasant voice. It was Boyston.

'Don't think much of your float,' he continued. 'A chocolate dinosaur? Pathetic!'

Boyston's gang, who seemed to find everything he said hilarious, all scoffed loudly.

'It looks even more pathetic than your stupid caramel giraffe,' said Boyston. 'Why do you bother?'

'We'd have won last year if it hadn't been for that cable,' protested Josh.

'Oh yeah? Well you didn't,' gloated Boyston. 'And there's no way on earth you'll beat our float this year either. It's a ten-metre-tall biscuit jar!'

'Well, we'll just have to see who wins,' said Josh, although even he had to admit Boyston's float sounded pretty cool.

#

Back at the Everyday Archaeological Museum, Gerard was finding his nights increasingly hard to cope with.

No wonder no one lasts long in this job, he thought as he stuffed more snacks into his mouth. The trouble was that the more he ate, the more his appetite grew, and Gerard had an appetite for one food item alone – the forbidden Amulet of Nutty Knitty. It seemed to be calling to him – beckoning, beckoning . . . But he had been warned to leave it alone and he certainly didn't want to set off the alarm and lose his job.

Instead he spent hours staring at the Amulet with a large sponge strapped strategically under his chin – to catch the endless flow of drool.

Then one night, disaster struck. It all started with the wrong jacket. It was a warm evening and Gerard had brought a different jacket to work, so when he reached into a secret pocket for a bite to eat, it was empty!

Gerard searched and searched every pocket.

'There's got to be a snack in here somewhere,' he said desperately. For although this wasn't his work jacket, all of Gerard's clothes contained at least one 'emergency' snack.

The more he searched, the more he thought about the Amulet. It was like a voice calling to him.

'*Come to me,*' murmured the Amulet. '*Eat me and you will discover sweetie pleasures beyond your wildest imaginings . . . you know you want to . . .*'

Finally, in despair, Gerard crawled into the room that contained the museum's most treasured item.

'One little bite, that's all I want,' he croaked. 'Nobody need ever know . . .'

With trembling hands he prised open the cabinet. Immediately alarms started going off and the sprinkler system rained down on him.

But even though bells were ringing and he was getting soaking wet, there it was, finally within his grasp . . . the cursed Amulet of Nutty Knitty!

Holding aloft the priceless artefact, Gerard shook with excitement.

'Lick? Bite? Nibble?' he mused. 'Nibble . . . that way it will last longer.'

Slowly he lifted the treat to his lips and then, unable to control himself, took a huge bite.

But before he could even start to savour the taste, the room went dark. There was a hideous fluttering noise: a strange, unsettling flapping of leathery wings and the sound of lips smacking . . .

'Get away from me!' squealed Gerard as his clothes were pulled and torn by what felt like hundreds of tiny mouths. And then just as suddenly as they had arrived the winged horrors were gone.

When the lights went back on, Gerard stood there naked
. . . but for his underpants.

'W-what w-were they and w-what did they w-want?' he
stammered.

Then he noticed on the pile of shredded clothes a single
empty chocolate wrapper.

'My chocolate snack! I knew I had one on me all along . . .'

7

Back in Josh's room, although they were busy getting ready for the Chocolate Festival, Josh couldn't stop thinking about the mysterious fall of the Chocolate Age.

'We need a translation of the curse on the Amulet of Nutty Knitty,' he said. 'Have you come up with anything, Spencer?'

'I'm afraid it's like no language I've ever seen,' Spencer replied. 'I think we're going to need some help.'

'To the sarcophagus!' said Josh.

As Zac Zoltan and Dr Brains emerged into the Mad Monster Agency, Odd Dan was happily dusting a filing cabinet. Even though he hated having his cleaning routine interrupted, he immediately stopped to help out.

'You need a Mad Monster language expert,' said Odd Dan, flicking though the Agency's files. They had contacts in just about every area of Mad Monster expertise from Mad Monster tracking to Mad Monster shopping habits and many more.

'Aha!' said Odd Dan, holding up a Fact File.

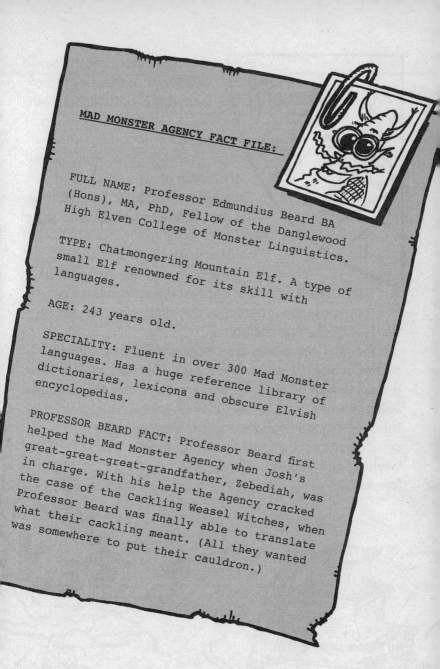

MAD MONSTER AGENCY FACT FILE:

FULL NAME: Professor Edmundius Beard BA
(Hons), MA, PhD, Fellow of the Danglewood
High Elven College of Monster Linguistics.

TYPE: Chatmongering Mountain Elf. A type of
small Elf renowned for its skill with
languages.

AGE: 243 years old.

SPECIALITY: Fluent in over 300 Mad Monster
languages. Has a huge reference library of
dictionaries, lexicons and obscure Elvish
encyclopedias.

PROFESSOR BEARD FACT: Professor Beard first
helped the Mad Monster Agency when Josh's
great-great-great-grandfather, Zebediah, was
in charge. With his help the Agency cracked
the case of the Cackling Weasel Witches, when
Professor Beard was finally able to translate
what their cackling meant. (All they wanted
was somewhere to put their cauldron.)

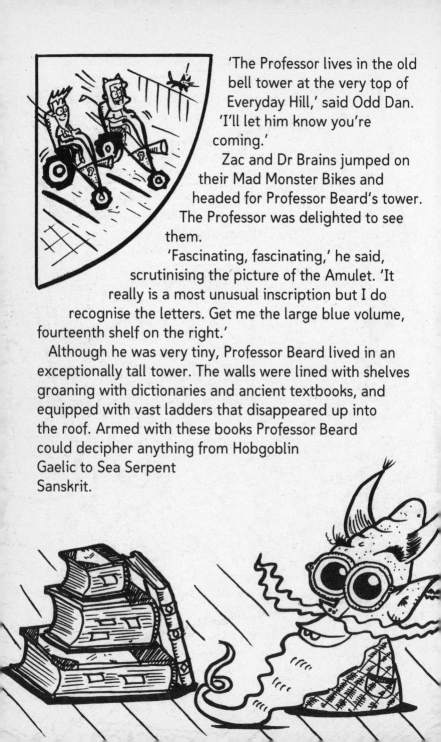

'The Professor lives in the old bell tower at the very top of Everyday Hill,' said Odd Dan. 'I'll let him know you're coming.'

Zac and Dr Brains jumped on their Mad Monster Bikes and headed for Professor Beard's tower. The Professor was delighted to see them.

'Fascinating, fascinating,' he said, scrutinising the picture of the Amulet. 'It really is a most unusual inscription but I do recognise the letters. Get me the large blue volume, fourteenth shelf on the right.'

Although he was very tiny, Professor Beard lived in an exceptionally tall tower. The walls were lined with shelves groaning with dictionaries and ancient textbooks, and equipped with vast ladders that disappeared up into the roof. Armed with these books Professor Beard could decipher anything from Hobgoblin Gaelic to Sea Serpent Sanskrit.

Zac passed the Professor his book. As he flicked avidly through the pages, Zac couldn't help but wonder how someone as tiny as Professor Beard, even with the help of ladders, could get such big books down from the shelves on his own.

'Yes, yes, I think I may have deciphered your Amulet's inscription,' he said after what seemed like an age.

'Really?' said Zac. 'What does it mean?'

'What we appear to have is some ancient form of Transylvanian . . .' said Professor Beard.

'I can't read it,' said Dr Brains.

'That's because you don't speak Ancient Gothenese,' said Professor Beard. 'This isn't an English dictionary . . .'

'So what does it mean?' asked Zac.

'Well, my Gothenese is a bit rusty,' said Professor Beard. 'But I think a pretty good translation would be: "He who eats of the Amulet —" er, let me see, "will Unleash a Sweet-Toothed Horde to —" um, yes I think this is right, "lay Waste to All Mankind!"'

'I've got a feeling we may be encountering this "horde" sooner rather than later,' said Zac ominously.

And he wasn't wrong . . .

8

Although he didn't realise it at the time, Gerard had indeed unleashed the formidable Curse of the Amulet of Nutty Knitty! What had stripped him to his pants in search of the concealed chocolate bar were none other than the fiendish CHOCOHOLIC VAMPIRES!!! And they hadn't had so much as a sniff of chocolate for hundreds of years. As they fluttered out of the museum, Everyday was about to find out what that meant . . .

Within an hour, the Vampires had nibbled through the alarm system wires, and consumed every single piece of chocolate in the museum. They had then regrouped at the top of the largest tree in the museum's garden. After having tasted the sweet flavour of chocolate for the first time in centuries, the Chocoholic Vampires wanted more – much, much more. It wouldn't be long before they were ready to strike again – and harder!

'Free at last, my sweet-eating friends!' It was Coco von Nibbling, leader of the Vampires.

'It's been so long,' said Chocco Nut-Guzzler, the largest of the flock. 'Me is *hungry*!'

The other Vampires all flapped their wings in approval– they too were hungry. Very, *very* hungry . . .

'We need more treats,' said Coco, scanning the horizon. 'Let us see what the foolish humans of this town have for us . . .'

'Me like the treats,' salivated Chocco. He then started snorting deeply, searching out even the merest whiff of chocolate. All the Vampires now joined in, sniffing the air, but, as always, Chocco's nose was first on the trail.

'Me can smell a choc ice not far from here!' beamed Chocco. 'The yummy yummy choc ice is *good* . . .'

'It certainly is,' cried Coco von Nibbling. 'It's time to feast! Then we must find a more permanent home . . . from where we can rule over this tasty earthling planet FOR EVER!!!'

The tree shuddered as the Chocoholic Vampires flapped into action, and they were soon homing in on their second chocolate-bearing victim.

9

When head guide Irma Sneef turned up for work the next day, she discovered Gerard Snax in his underpants and the Amulet of Nutty Knitty gone.

'I c-c-couldn't help myself,' blubbered Gerard. 'The Amulet was c-c-calling me.'

'But what happened to your clothes?' Irma asked.

'It was the creatures . . . I couldn't do anything about it,' whined Gerard. 'They wanted my chocolate bar – the one I keep hidden in my Secret Choccy Pocket.'

'Creatures . . . seeking chocolate? What complete nonsense!' scoffed Mrs Sneef, before adding menacingly, 'But you must tell no one about what has happened here. Understood?'

But it was too late – the Amulet had been nibbled. And strange and disturbing things began happening all over town . . .

A man walking past the museum was bundled roughly to the ground. When he got up he discovered his choc ice had been savaged.

Later an old lady about to have a cup of hot chocolate was pinned against a wall, heard a loud slurp and discovered her drink had been ravaged.

A woman waiting for a night bus was about to sample a chocolate eclair when a scaly hand tripped her up. Before she could get to her feet her cake was brutally snatched.

A dog woke up to find his kennel in tatters and his chocolate treats gone – snuffled down by mysterious visitors!

Gerard Snax had unleashed something horrible,
something disgusting, something downright greedy . . .

10

As stories of these chocolate assaults started to filter
through to the school playground, Josh and Spencer quickly
realised that their worst fears had come true.

And although many kids had heard about the mysterious treat-eating creatures, Boyston's voice was, as usual, the loudest.

'Listen up, everyone, I had a close encounter of the spooky kind last night!' he boomed to the whole playground. 'I was just about to have a chocolate sundae when the creatures appeared. They crept up on me like cowards. They should have known not to mess with Boyston Fitch.'

'So what did you do?' asked Josh. 'Did you catch them?'
'Well, I would have if it hadn't been so late at night,'
bragged Boyston. 'But I gave them a fright.'
'It must have been the sight of you in your pyjamas!'
chuckled Spencer.

'No it wasn't!' said Boyston. 'For your information, I didn't
have my Mad Monster net with me. But don't you worry,
they won't get away with it next time. In fact me and the
boys are going on a Mad Monster hunt tonight!'

Boyston and his gang fancied themselves as Mad Monster Agents, and often got in the way of Zac and Dr Brains (although of course they didn't know it was actually Josh and Spencer). Their approach to Mad Monster hunting involved sticks and nets – but it didn't stop them boasting about their 'skills'.

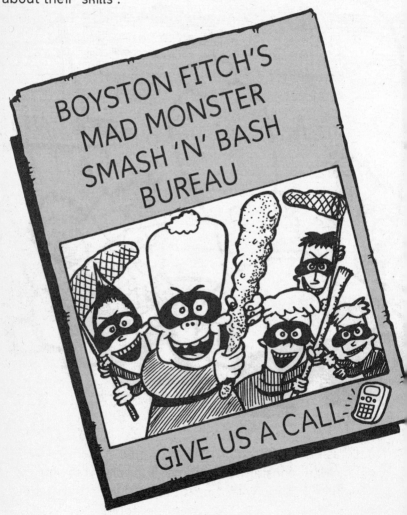

Before Boyston could bore everyone with the details of his hunt, the school bell rang. The Headmistress had a special announcement for the whole school.

As you may know, there appears to be a spate of terrifying chocolate-related robberies. And with the annual Chocolate Festival taking place later this week, it has been decided that extra security measures are needed to protect the floats . . . They will all be kept under lock and key in the school sports hall. And will only be put in position in the town centre at the last minute on the morning of the Festival.

The rest of the day passed very slowly for Josh and Spencer – they couldn't wait to get back to the Agency.

But when they got home their path was blocked – by Josh's mother . . .

Josh was going to complain, but could tell that his mother was in one of her not-to-be-argued-with moods!

11

Josh and Spencer wolfed down the salad and when they got to Josh's room they weren't surprised to see that the eyes on Josh's great-great-great-grandfather's walking stick were glowing red . . .

'Time to get busy!' said Josh as they made for the trapdoor and slid down into the secret room below.

When they emerged into the Agency as Zac Zoltan and Dr Brains, they couldn't believe what was waiting for them.

On every screen were frightened people, some holding empty chocolate boxes, some broken cake stands, many with ripped clothes.

Odd Dan was frantically pressing buttons as more and more reports poured in.

'Phew, thank goodness you're here,' he said to Zac. 'Looks like there's been a major outbreak of Mad Monster activity. The Mad Monster Mainframe has gone ballistic!'

Zac and Dr Brains sat behind the desk to see for themselves. Odd Dan turned up the sound on an elderly lady clutching an empty jar.

Every person had a similar tale to tell – chocolate bars decimated, bags of sweets devastated and entire cakes annihilated.

Zac turned to Odd Dan and Dr Brains. It was time for Zac Zoltan's Mad Monster Agency to act.

'We seem to have a full-blown Mad Monster Crisis on our hands,' said Zac. 'We need to get a closer look at one of these critters. Only when we've identified them can we formulate a Mad Monster Plan.'

'Yes, but where are we going to find one?' asked Dr Brains.

'Let's begin with sweet shops and ice-cream stands and take it from there,' said Zac.

Zac and Dr Brains spent the evening frantically searching Everyday on their Mad Monster Bikes, but the monsters always seemed to be at least one step ahead of them. At least Boyston Fitch and his mob, who they'd bumped into twice, weren't having any more luck and had called it a night. But Zac wasn't going to give up so easily.

'They must have a secret hideaway somewhere,' said Zac. 'Where would you go after you'd stuffed yourself with stolen chocolate?'

'We know they can fly, so maybe they chose somewhere high up and out of the way,' said Dr Brains. 'But we've been to all the tall buildings in town tonight.'

'Not quite all of them,' said Zac excitedly. 'Where's the highest place in Everyday?'

'Professor Beard's tower!' said Dr Brains.

'Exactly!' said Zac.

It was pitch dark when they arrived at Professor Beard's. They had to knock and knock before eventually he answered, looking rather flustered.

'The most confounded thing,' said Professor Beard. 'I was researching the Amulet of Nutty Knitty when my chocolate biscuit vanished!'

'Sounds like our old friends,' said Zac.

'Well, ever since it happened there have been all kinds of strange noises coming from the very top of the tower,' said Professor Beard. 'I'm much too scared to go up there. I called you on the Mad Monster hotline, but Odd Dan told me you were out on a mission already.'

'So that's where they're hiding out!' said Zac. 'We need to see what we're dealing with here. I'm going up!'

'They won't take kindly to being disturbed,' said Dr Brains. 'Be careful.'

With Dr Brains and Professor Beard waiting nervously below, Zac made his way to the very top of the tower. As he slowly climbed the rickety stairs and ladders, he became increasingly aware of fluttering wings and strange squeaks. Then, finally, he caught his first glimpse. Frozen in the beam from his torch and clustered together like the nuts in a bar of Super-Nut-o-Choc was a flock of drooling winged creatures. Zac was face to face with the CHOCOHOLIC VAMPIRES!

And more worryingly, *they* had seen *him*.

'We seem to have a visitor!' said Coco von Nibbling.

'Me can't smell chocolate,' said Chocco Nut-Guzzler disappointedly.

At first they fluttered down, but because Zac wasn't carrying anything edible they quickly flapped away again.

'*Bad* chocolate!' said Chocco. 'Me no likey . . .'

'Leave our abode at once, intruder!' said Coco.

'Your days are numbered, Vampires!' said Zac defiantly. 'Zac Zoltan's Mad Monster Agency is on your tail!'

'You'll never stop us!' cackled Coco. 'NEVER!'

13

Zac quickly clambered down from the top of the tower. He
had seen enough.

'Chocoholic Vampires!' he said, as soon as he was back on
the ground. 'I should have known. These creatures have an
unquenchable thirst for all things chocolatey.'

'Of course!' said Dr Brains. 'Good thing you weren't
carrying any chocolate – they would have been all over you
like a winged rash.'

'So that's what was in the tower!' said Professor Beard. 'An infestation of Chocoholic Vampires. I keep some of my most valuable books up there – they could be ruined.'

'Unless they're made of chocolate, they won't be touched,' said Dr Brains reassuringly.

'Yes, but what about the guano?' said Professor Beard. 'Chocolate guano is highly toxic.'

'Guano?' asked Zac.

'It's the scientific name for bat-poo,' said Dr Brains. '*Guano* is a word derived from the native peoples of –'

'We don't have time for this,' said Zac. 'We have to stop these critters!'

'I have found something that could help you,' said Professor Beard, handing Zac a piece of paper. 'It's what I was looking for when my biscuit vanished.'

'It looks like a recipe,' said Zac.

'Yes, for the Amulet of Nutty Knitty,' said Professor Beard. 'It was at the back of my oldest book of life-saving recipes. Odd Dan should have no problem making one of these.'

With the recipe safely tucked in his pocket, Zac zoomed back to the Agency with Dr Brains. It was time to come up with a plan. Odd Dan searched the Fact Files until he came up with the one they needed – an ancient-looking file on crumbling, yellowed parchment.

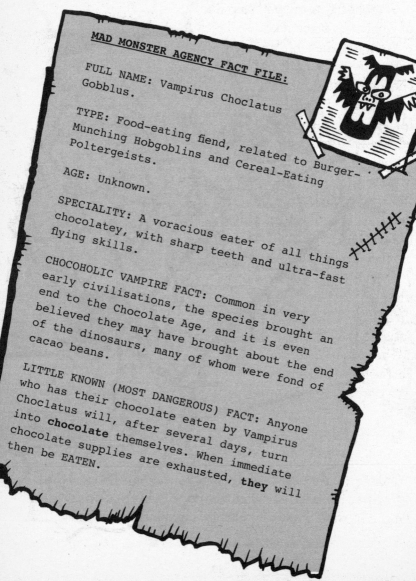

MAD MONSTER AGENCY FACT FILE:

FULL NAME: Vampirus Choclatus Gobblus.

TYPE: Food-eating fiend, related to Burger-Munching Hobgoblins and Cereal-Eating Poltergeists.

AGE: Unknown.

SPECIALITY: A voracious eater of all things chocolatey, with sharp teeth and ultra-fast flying skills.

CHOCOHOLIC VAMPIRE FACT: Common in very early civilisations, the species brought an end to the Chocolate Age, and it is even believed they may have brought about the end of the dinosaurs, many of whom were fond of cacao beans.

LITTLE KNOWN (MOST DANGEROUS) FACT: Anyone who has their chocolate eaten by Vampirus Choclatus will, after several days, turn into **chocolate** themselves. When immediate chocolate supplies are exhausted, **they** will then be EATEN.

'Now we know what happened to the Chocolate Age people. They turned into chocolate . . . and . . .' said Zac, his voice tailing off. He didn't want to think of what took place next.

'Well, they haven't exhausted all supplies of chocolate *yet*. From my knowledge of Mad Monsters of the hungry variety,' mused Odd Dan, nibbling on a breadstick, 'they tend to start off with the easy pickings: old ladies, shops, that kind of thing. Then . . .'

'Then what?' asked Zac.

'Then they go for the big pig-out,' said Odd Dan. 'Something that *really* satisfies their appetite.'

'The Annual Chocolate Festival!' said Dr Brains. 'We don't have long!'

14

When Gerard Snax returned home after the incident at the museum, he was still shaken, but was even more shocked by what he found when he opened the door. . .

'My jackets!' wailed Gerard. Every single one had been torn to shreds and all that was left of his snacks were empty wrappers.

But things were about to get even worse for Gerard. A few days later he began feeling unwell and when he looked in the mirror he got the fright of his life . . .

'My face,' he spluttered. 'What *are* these things?!?'

Gerard's face was covered in . . . nuts and raisins!

'What's going on?!' he blubbered. 'And what's happened to my hair?'

Where once Gerard had a thick head of hair, in its place was something pink, sticky and sweet.

'It's turned into candy floss!'

He immediately called an ambulance.

At the hospital he was alarmed to see other people in a similar condition. One lady's nose had turned into toffee. A bald man's head was covered in hundreds and thousands.

A doctor approached Gerard and immediately sent him to have a blood test.

When the doctor eventually returned with the results, the news was terrifying.

'Your blood seems to be turning into something sweet, brown and sticky,' said the doctor. 'It appears to be turning into, er, how can I put this . . . chocolate milkshake!'

'What's happening to me?' snivelled Gerard.

'I'm sorry to say, Mr Snax,' said the doctor, 'but just like all the other patients out there . . . you're turning into chocolate!!!'

But as Gerard Snax contemplated life as a chocolate, his only hope, the Mad Monster Agency, was ready to strike back.

15

With the Mad Monster Mainframe screens full of people turning into chocolate the Agency was now on Monster Code Red.

'We need to set a trap,' said Zac. 'The biggest trap the Mad Monster Agency has ever set.'

'A trap?' said Odd Dan.

'Yes, the only way to stop the Vampires is to trap them in a giant urn sealed with an Amulet of Nutty Knitty,' said Zac. 'When the curse is recited, they will disappear for ever and everyone will return to normal . . .'

'We're dealing with pretty tough Mad Monsters here,' he continued. 'And unless we stop them, Everyday and the rest of mankind could go the way of the people of the Chocolate Age.'
'And *they* came to a pretty sticky end,' said Odd Dan grimly.

Dr Brains had been madly tapping at his calculator.
'By my calculations we only have a few hours to save the residents of Everyday from becoming Vampire food,' he said.

'The annual Chocolate Festival will provide us with the perfect cover,' said Zac. 'Even though the Vampires mainly operate at night, it will be too tempting for them to resist. We're going to need an Amulet of Nutty Knitty. How's Professor Beard's recipe going?'

'Well, it's in the oven as we speak,' said Odd Dan. 'Although it was a real job tracking down all the ingredients.'

'Great,' said Zac. 'I also need you to make the bait – do you think you can make something so chocolatey that the Vampires will be powerless to resist?'

'Do levitating octopuses have twelve legs?' said Odd Dan.

'So now we have a trap,' said Dr Brains. 'But what about the urn? We're going to need one that's huge.'

'And who do we know who's built a massive biscuit jar?' chuckled Zac.

'Boyston Fitch! Of course!' said Dr Brains.

'In the interest of saving Everyday we're going to have to "borrow" Boyston's Chocolate Festival float,' said Zac. 'We'll also take the Chocosaurus – it will make a great hideout. We need to get them now. We must be in position before the rest of the floats arrive.'

While Zac made his final preparations, Odd Dan got to work finishing the Amulet of Nutty Knitty and making the super-tasty bait. Dr Brains, meanwhile, went to his workbench. With his Brain Helmet set on hyper-drive he made the final adjustments to his latest gadget – a chocoholic-busting device he'd been working on since their first encounter with the Vampires.

When everything was ready, Zac, Brains and Odd Dan
finally made for the Mad Monstermobile.
'It's weird going to school so late at night!' said Zac.
'I'm quite looking forward to it,' said Dr Brains. 'I've often
dreamt of breaking in after hours to do some extra work!'

16

All was quiet at Everyday School when they arrived.

'OK, Odd Dan, get the Monstermobile as close to the sports hall as possible,' said Zac.

Odd Dan moved the van into position. But as they pulled up, something wasn't right. The sports hall door was ajar and there was light coming from inside!

'Oh no!' said Zac. 'Looks like the Chocoholic Vampires have got here first!'

'Don't worry!' said Dr Brains. 'This is the perfect chance to try out my gadget.'

He unveiled a large piece of equipment that looked like a giant toothpaste tube. 'Behold! The Tactical Ordnance Overpowering Terminating Homogeniser . . . or TOOTH for short.' Like most of Dr Brains' gadgets its initials were easier to remember than its actual name.

'Interesting,' said Zac, admiring the device.

'It fires out a constant stream of fluoride-enriched unguent . . .' said Dr Brains.

'You mean toothpaste?' said Zac.

'Exactly!' said Dr Brains triumphantly.

'Brilliant!' said Zac. 'If there's one thing a Mad Monster with a sweet tooth loathes above everything else it's toothpaste!'

Dr Brains was happy inventing gadgets, but he wasn't so keen on using them. Instead that honour went to Zac, so with Zac in control of the TOOTH, it was time to get to work. Odd Dan deployed the Mad Monstermobile winch, lowering Zac and Dr Brains over the school wall.

'Can you see anything?' whispered Dr Brains, anxiously.

96

'They won't go for us unless someone's got a piece of chocolate on them,' said Zac reassuringly.

They proceeded into the hall, and what they saw had nothing to do with Mad Monsters . . . but it was almost as sinister!

It was Boyston Fitch and his gang – and they were about to sabotage Josh and Spencer's float!

'Step away from that float!' said Zac. 'We're here on important Mad Monster business and you are interfering with our mission.'

'Well, if it isn't the great Zac Zoltan,' mocked Boyston. 'Sneaking around in a school gym – is that really the best you can do?'

As Zac looked around he suddenly realised they were surrounded by Boyston's gang . . .

'We couldn't find any Mad Monsters, so we thought we'd liven up the evening by "customising" the float made by those pathetic losers Josh Flunk and Spencer Topps,' said Boyston. 'But since you and your little helpers turned up, things look like they're going to get a lot more interesting around here anyway!'

'Activate the TOOTH,' whispered Dr Brains.

Zac pulled the lever, squirting out a stream of sticky toothpaste.

Boyston stopped for a second, looking at the puddle of
toothpaste in front of them.

'I think I need to boost the squirt levels,' whispered Dr
Brains.

'Toothpaste?!?' guffawed Boyston.

As the gang closed in, they noticed something strange
about Boyston — his hair was starting to look shiny and
edible, and his face all nutty.

'I think Boyston is turning into chocolate!' murmured Zac.

'What's going on?' blubbered Boyston, looking down. 'My hands, they're made of . . . chocolate marzipan!' The rest of the gang stopped in their tracks.

'Stop it!' shrieked Boyston.

'Looks like the Chocoholic Vampires got to you before you got to them,' said Zac. 'I think you should get to a hospital, Boyston . . . and leave the Mad Monster work to us.'

Boyston and his gang fled the sports hall, screaming like babies.

17

With Boyston and his mob off the scene, the Mad Monster Agency soon had the two floats attached to the back of the Monstermobile.

'Amateurs!' said Zac. 'That'll teach him not to mess with Mad Monsters.'

'We need to get these in position in the town square,' said Odd Dan as they pulled away.

'And fast,' added Dr Brains.

When they arrived in the town centre, it was all quiet and deserted.

It was time for the Mad Monster Agency to set their trap.
First the huge biscuit jar was put into position.
'Great! Now for the bait,' said Zac. 'What have you got,
Odd Dan?'

'I should warn you that there has been a last-minute adjustment to the bait plan,' interrupted Dr Brains.

'*Adjustment*? What kind of an adjustment?' asked Zac nervously.

'I did some final calculations and to have the best chance of catching all the Vampires,' continued Dr Brains, '*you're* going to have to "wear" the bait! I came up with another gadget . . .'

18

Odd Dan reached into the back of the van and held up an outfit made of an edible fabric.

'Behold the Irresistible Super-Sweet Totally Toothsome Confectionery Costume or ISSTTCC for short,' said Dr Brains proudly. 'Odd Dan followed my design perfectly!'

'I think we'll call it the Chocolate Suit,' said Zac.

'And don't worry about getting turned into chocolate yourself,' said Dr Brains reassuringly. 'The inner layer is one hundred per cent Vampire-proof.'

'It certainly smells good,' said Zac, trying not to think about being nibbled at by Vampires.

'It's made out of my secret recipe for quadruple-chocolate brownies,' said Odd Dan.

'The ones that come with a dentist's warning?' said Zac, who avoided Odd Dan's brownies because they gave him toothache.

'The very same,' said Odd Dan proudly. 'But with extra fudge topping. If that doesn't attract the Chocoholic Vampires, then nothing will.'

'It's a bit tight, but it fits,' said Zac, squeezing into the suit.

'Let's just hope those Chocoholic Vampires don't get carried away and eat through the safety layer!'

Zac was all set to get into position in the biscuit jar and he had TOOTH at the ready to blast any stragglers into the jar.

'Have you got a clear view of the biscuit jar?' shouted Zac to Dr Brains, who had taken up his position in the float.

'Affirmative,' said Dr Brains, his face just visible through one of the dinosaur's eyes.

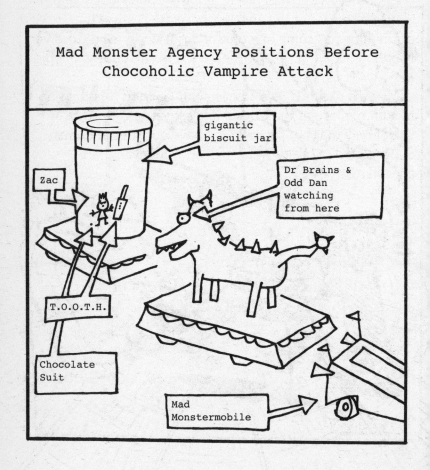

With the Mad Monster Agency team in position the trap was set. All they had to do was wait . . .

19

Early in the morning, excited townsfolk started to arrive for the parade. As Zac had predicted, the Chocoholic Vampires were well aware of the annual Chocolate Festival too.

'The time has come, my gluttonous friends,' said Coco von Nibbling, high in Professor Beard's tower. 'Today is the big day.'

'Me is so excited,' said Chocco Nut-Guzzler. 'Me is going to stuff me face at the Chocolate Festival.'

'Not only that but soon we will have our special human Super-Vampire,' said Coco, 'to lead us to even more chocolate!!!'

Soon the air was black with Vampires, with one thing on their minds – CHOCOLATE!

As they approached the Festival, Chocco Nut-Guzzler was getting excited.

'Me can smell *really* good chocolate,' said Chocco. 'Me is talking the really, really good stuff!'

The Vampires flapped faster – this was the feast they had been waiting thousands of years for . . .

'Soon the world will be ours!' drooled Coco.

20

Meanwhile, in the town centre, Zac and the crew waited tensely . . .

'I can feel them coming,' said Odd Dan, who despite being a giant Troll always got nervous when he was actually confronted by other monsters.

'Chocoholic Vampires approaching!' whispered Dr Brains.

'Ready for action,' replied Zac.

Then, all of a sudden, they swarmed in – hundreds of them
... drooling and gobbling at Zac's Chocolate Suit. Zac
waved his arms around to attract them into the jar.

'Me like this brownie,' exclaimed Chocco. The Vampires were fighting over Zac to get at Odd Dan's quadruple-chocolate brownies.

'Leave some for me,' said Coco.

As Zac used TOOTH to blast the last stragglers into the jar, he realised he didn't have much time – the Vampires would soon gobble their way through his suit. Jumping out, he balanced on the rim of the biscuit jar.

'Now!' shouted Zac. 'The lid!'

Odd Dan threw Zac the lid, which he slammed down as hard as possible – the Vampires were trapped. But as Zac turned away in triumph he felt a tug on his leg – Coco von Nibbling and Chocco Nut-Guzzler had slipped out.

'Activate TOOTH!' cried Dr Brains as Zac wrestled with the fanged fiends.

Once again Zac Zoltan unleashed TOOTH . . . There was a loud squelching noise and a stream of fluoride toothpaste sprayed out . . .

'Me no likey!' wailed Chocco, jumping back. 'What is this stuff???'

'Toothpaste!' screamed Coco, dodging the spray of fluoride.

But Coco and Chocco were too quick and Zac just could not get a direct hit. When he finally ran out of toothpaste, they turned on him.

'Ha ha!' cackled Coco. 'The game's up!'

'Me want a bitey of him,' drooled Chocco.

'Odd Dan – time for some Kung Food!' shouted Zac urgently as the Vampires loomed, fangs bared.

'The overhead cable,' said Dr Brains, remembering what had happened to their chocolate giraffe the year before. 'It's our only chance!' Odd Dan and Dr Brains jumped out of the chocolate dinosaur.

'Now!' shouted Zac.

KAZABAZOOLY!

Odd Dan let out a ground-shaking cry – it was time for some Kung-Food. The furious Troll stunned the Vampires with a craftily thrown cracker, before shoving the float with a flying spinning kick.

'Duck!' shouted Dr Brains as the float careered towards the cable.

There was a loud fizzing noise as the Chocosaurus struck the cable – melting chocolate poured down on to Coco and Chocco. They simply couldn't resist the delicious mixture, and were so busy guzzling that Zac finally had his chance to grab them.

Scooping up the two helpless, sticky Vampires, Zac tossed them in the jar and sealed it once and for all.

21

'Trapped!' cried Odd Dan. 'That was close! But it's another triumph for Zac Zoltan's Mad Monster Agency!'

All the townsfolk, who had been cowering behind stalls and cars, emerged cheering and clapping.

'Great work, guys!' said Zac. 'But we're not quite done. Now we've got to seal them in.'

Dr Brains arrived holding aloft the new Amulet of Nutty Knitty.

'I'm not too sure of the pronunciation,' said Dr Brains, 'but I hope this works.'

Dr Brains recited the curse on the Amulet to seal them in. 'Knit Nutty, Nut Knitty, Nut, Nut, NUTS!'

There was a loud fizzing noise and inside the jar the Vampires' eyes drooped shut and they fell instantly into a deep sleep!

'They'll be quite happy dreaming of chocolate,' said Odd Dan. 'And everyone who was bitten should slowly start to return to normal.'

'Let's just hope they don't wake up again for a long, long time!' said Dr Brains.

But as the Mad Monster Agency team shook hands and congratulated each other, they suddenly noticed that the crowd had stopped applauding. Looming over the town was something large, scary and decidedly chocolatey.

'I'm sorry,' said Odd Dan anxiously. 'I really hoped it wouldn't come to this. The Chocoholic Vampires can select one of their victims to become a Super-Vampire . . .'

'Super-Vampire?' said Dr Brains. Boyston Fitch was trouble at his normal size, but as big as a house and a Vampire? This was a bit too much to handle.

'Yes, to help them locate more chocolate supplies,' continued Odd Dan. 'And the Super-Vampire's sense of smell and appetite will be the greatest of them all!'

The huge Boyston Fitch was
gobbling everything in his
path, smashing up stalls
and scattering terrified
people in all directions.

'We've got to stop him!'
said Zac.

'But how?' said Odd Dan.

'The TOOTH's out of
ammo,' said Dr Brains.

CHOMP!
MUNCH!

The Mad Monster Agency had to come up with something and fast, or mankind was still doomed!

'We need toothpaste, we need mouthwash, we need everything that a sweet tooth doesn't,' said Dr Brains. 'But where are we going to find that?'

Then Zac started to smile. 'Somewhere really boring, that's where!'

'What do you mean?' asked Dr Brains.

'Remember the school trip to the town's conference centre?' said Zac.

'Of course,' said Dr Brains.

'Well, there's a dentists' conference taking place there now,' said Zac. '*They'll* have the gear to sort out Boyston!'

23

'We need to lure him to the conference centre at once!' said Zac. 'We've still got the bottom half of the dinosaur float – that might do it!'

They quickly attached what was left of the Chocosaurus to the back of the van.

'Let's get moving!' said Zac.

'Boyston is right on our tail!' said Dr Brains as they headed for the conference centre.

THUMP!

Odd Dan tried his best to keep the giant Vampire at arms length, but Boyston had still managed to grab a few chunks of the chocolate dinosaur . . . and was gaining on them.

'Nearly there,' said Zac. 'Not much longer . . .'

'Put your foot down, Odd Dan! Let's go turbo!' said Dr Brains. 'Good thing I boosted the Mad Monstermobile!'

The Mad Monstermobile zoomed straight into the middle of the conference centre. As Boyston Fitch finally got his hands on the chocolate dinosaur, and started scoffing it greedily, Zac had to mobilise terrified dentists at once.

'Listen up, everyone,' said Zac at the top of his voice. 'Grab whatever dentist's tools you've got and follow me. If you don't, we're all doomed to become Chocoholic Vampire cuisine!'

Zac, Dr Brains and Odd Dan picked up the drills and toothpaste tubes nearest them and led the dentists outside.

Behind them Boyston Fitch had finished eating the dinosaur
float and had started sniffing the air for more.
  'He won't find any chocolate here!' chuckled Zac.

There was no time to lose. Zac, armed with the biggest bottle of mouthwash he could find, led the charge.

'Ok, dentists, get to work!' he cried.

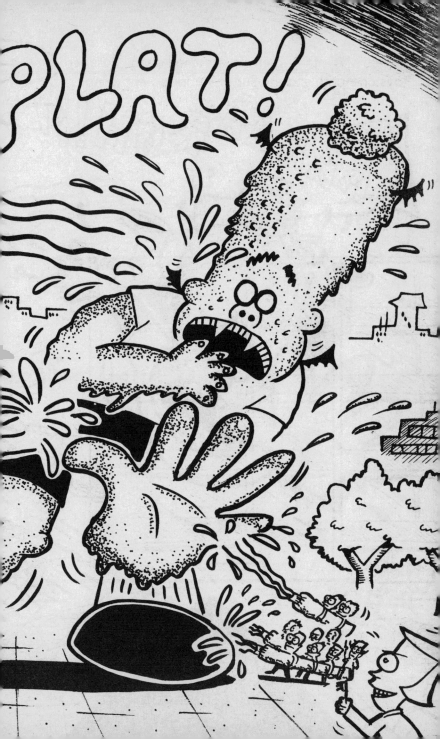

A team of dental hygienists stretched dental floss across Boyston's path and the Super-Vampire went flying!

'It's working!' said Dr Brains as they watched Boyston start to shrink. 'The teeth-cleaning devices are stronger than chocolate!'

When the dentists and the Mad Monster team pulled back, they revealed a normal-sized and rather confused-looking Boyston.

Although he didn't look *quite* normal. His face was still a little nutty, and his hands were puffy and marshmallow-like. He also looked rather embarrassed – dressed only in rags.

But thanks to Zac Zoltan's Mad Monster Agency, the world was once again safe from the fearsome fangs of the Chocoholic Vampires!

After the dust settled, at the Mad Monster Agency the team was finally able to relax.

'Savoury muffin, anyone?' said Odd Dan. 'I don't think I'll be making brownies for a while!'

'I think I'll pass,' said Dr Brains.

'I've lost my appetite,' chuckled Zac.

Even if they would never look at chocolate the same way again, the Agency could console themselves on a job well done.

The Chocoholic Vampires were gone, buried in a biscuit jar deep beneath the Everyday Archaeological Museum.

New super-stringent security measures were put in place to make sure no one ever got near the museum's artefacts again. To be extra safe Mr and Mrs Sneef even did the night shift themselves.

As soon as the last Vampire had disappeared people started to recover and turn back into humans – even Gerard Snax, who decided he'd never eat another chocolate again.

And Boyston Fitch, well, he returned to being his normal annoying self. Although now he hurries past sweet shops . . .

CASE CLOSED

But back at the Agency, the eyes on the ivory skull of Zebadiah Zoltan's favourite walking stick started to glow red . . . Time for another mission for Zac Zoltan's Mad Monster Agency!

BONUS FEATURES

The Mad Monster History of The
World Part I:
The Chocolate Age
(in bite-size pieces)

At home with the Chocoholic
Vampires

Odd Dan's Super-Sweet Recipe

Inside the Mad Monster Agency

Dr Brains' Gizmo Corner

The Chocolate Age (in bite-size pieces)

After the Bronze Age there was a period of great turmoil, with numerous tribes vying for prominence. Amongst these was the much feared **Soup Clan**, the first people to discover the warming benefits of boiled down vegetables . . .

The terrifying **Pie Tribe**, who were the first to blend pastry with tasty, nutritious fillings . . .

And then there were the **Chocolate People** – laid-back, sweet-toothed pacifists who liked nothing better than to eat chocolatey treats all day. Unfortunately, they had to constantly fight off their more aggressive neighbours until a charismatic man emerged as their leader – the good **Chief Bonbon the First** . . .

Through the power of his rhetoric and his irresistible chocolates, Chief Bonbon was eventually able to unite the warring peoples – and create a Chocolate Utopia known as the **Chocolate Age** . . .

However, as the Chocolate People basked in an era of plenty, little did they know that evil forces were plotting to take everything from them. **Chocoholic Vampires** – the scourge of all sweet-toothed peoples – descended in huge numbers, devouring all that was before them . . .

Although Chief Bonbon rallied his troops and fought shoulder to shoulder with the Soup Clan and the Pie Tribe, at the final encounter (the Battle of Chocolate Mountain) the Vampires proved too powerful . . .

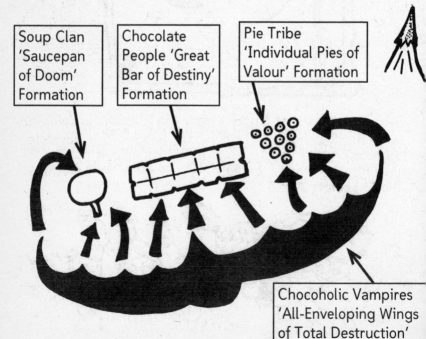

Soup Clan 'Saucepan of Doom' Formation

Chocolate People 'Great Bar of Destiny' Formation

Pie Tribe 'Individual Pies of Valour' Formation

Chocoholic Vampires 'All-Enveloping Wings of Total Destruction' Formation

With Chief Bonbon defeated, they were free to ravage the entire civilisation . . . The Chocolate Age was over – but with his dying breath Chief Bonbon summoned the ancient **Glutton-Witches of D'o-nutt** and commanded them to create a magic Amulet with the power to save mankind from destruction by the evil bats.

With the **Amulet of Nutty Knitty** the Chocoholic Vampires were finally banished – sadly all too late for the Chocolate Age. But thanks to Chief Bonbon, we enjoy delicious chocolatey snacks to this day . . .

AT HOME WITH THE CHOCOHOLIC VAMPIRES

In between banishments to the biscuit urn for the whole of eternity, we catch two famous Vampires 'at home' . . .

Tooth sharpener – for keeping those fangs extra pointy

Blackout blinds – to keep nasty daylight out

Cloak press – a well-ironed cloak is a must for any self-respecting Vampire

Padded perch – for the perfect day's sleep

Chocolate stash – for when the nibbles kick in

Wing-waxing kit – to ensure a smooth take-off at the drop of a sweetie wrapper

Odd Dan's Super-Sweet Recipe

- Take a large amount of chocolate, now add chocolate . . .

- Leave overnight then soak in chocolate sauce . . .

- Cover in chocolate sprinkles . . .

- Drizzle with chocolate . . .

- Now enjoy!

  (Make sure you have a toothbrush handy!)

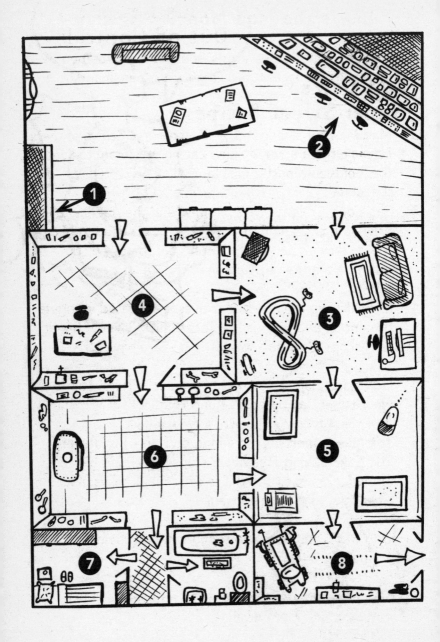

Inside the Mad Monster Agency

1   Cabinet of curiosities – gifts, souvenirs and mementos of past missions, including a goblin's toenail and a warlock's wart.

2   Mad Monster screens – the hi-tech nerve centre of the Agency, these screens allow Zac and his team to keep track of Mad Monster problems all over Everyday.

3   Zac's den – missions are planned and the Agency team briefed in Zac's home-from-home. Some deep thinking takes place on Zebadiah Zoltan's old, battered sofa – a gift from a grateful Ottoman vizier!

4   Dr Brains workshop – brainwaves are focused, gadgets dreamt up and gizmos fine-tuned in Dr Brains' chaotic workshop. (Only *he* knows where everything is!)

5   Odd Dan's dojo – watch out for flying fritters! This is where Odd Dan practises Kung Food.

6   The most important room for Odd Dan – his kitchen! The Cake-Baking Troll never stops perfecting his legendary recipes and this is where it all takes place. Check out that antique oven!

7   Odd Dan's bedroom and reinforced bathroom – Trolls are heavy!

8   Mad Monstermobile garage – for a quick exit when there's a Mad Monster alert.

Dr Brains' Gizmo Corner
The Brain-Booster Helmet

By tuning into my brainwaves the Brain-Booster Helmet turbo boosts them – making the wearer even smarter! Different attachments can be added, depending on the mission.

Many of them are still at the prototype stage like the **Chartmancer** (map-reading skills and sense of direction become super-charged).

Loony Lexicon (gives the wearer the ability to instantly translate certain Mad Monster languages).

The Inspirationaliser (which immediately takes an idea and turns it into genius).

For more Mad Monster Mayhem look out for . . .

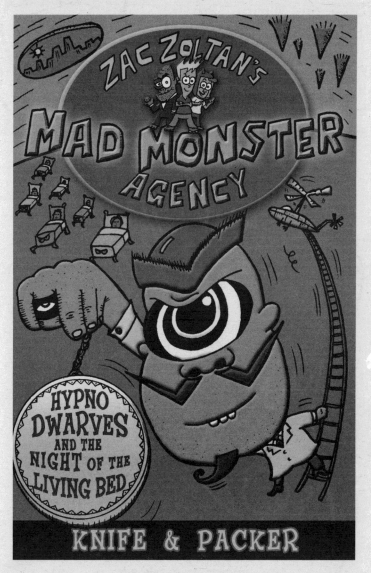

Available July 2009